Chief Red Horse Tells About Custer

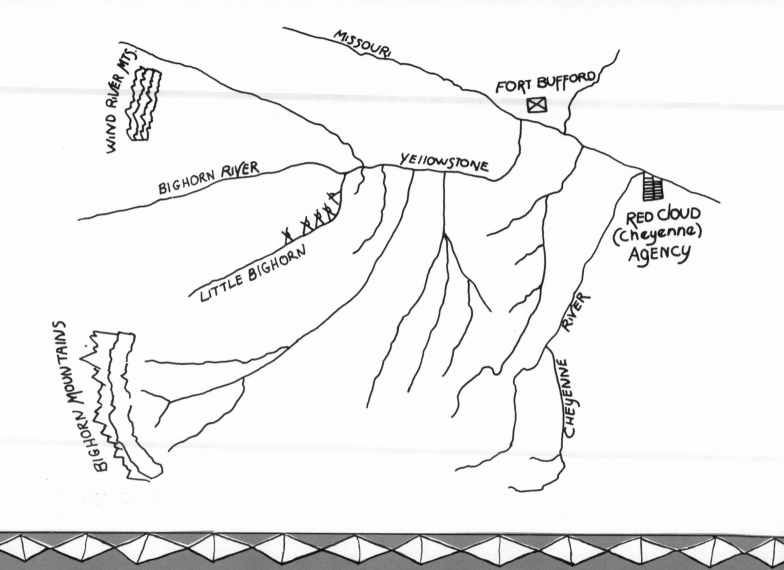

Chief Red Horse Tells About Custer

THE BATTLE OF THE LITTLE BIGHORN

AN EYEWITNESS ACCOUNT TOLD IN INDIAN SIGN LANGUAGE

Jessie Brewer McGaw

ELSEVIER/NELSON BOOKS · New York

The material used in this book — the Indian sign language and descriptions of the signs, as well as Chief Red Horse's drawings of the Battle of the Little Bighorn — have been used with the permission of the Smithsonian Institution, Washington, D.C.

Library of Congress Cataloging in Publication Data

McGaw, Jessie Brewer.
Chief Red Horse tells about Custer.
Based on diagrams and detailed descriptions of Red Horse's report as recorded by Dr. Charles E. McChesney, acting assistant surgeon of the U.S. Army.
Summary: Relates the account of the Battle of the Little Bighorn told five years later by Sioux Chief Red Horse, who fought in the conflict.
1. Little Big Horn, Battle of the,1876—Juvenile literature. 2. Custer, George Armstrong, 1839–1876— Juvenile literature. 3. Indians of North America— Sign language—Juvenile literature. 4. Red Horse, Chief—Juvenile literature. [1. Little Big Horn, Battle of the, 1876. 2. Custer, George Armstrong, 1839- 1876. 3. Indians of North America—Sign language. 4. Red Horse, Chief] I. Red Horse, Chief. II. McChesney, Charles E. III. Title.
E83.876.M37   973.8'2   81-1392
ISBN 0-525-66713-X   AACR2

Published in the United States by
Elsevier-Dutton Publishing Co., Inc., New York, N.Y. 10016.
Published simultaneously in Don Mills, Ontario, by Nelson/Canada.
Printed in the U.S.A.   First edition
10 9 8 7 6 5 4 3 2 1

TO NANCY AND ROB

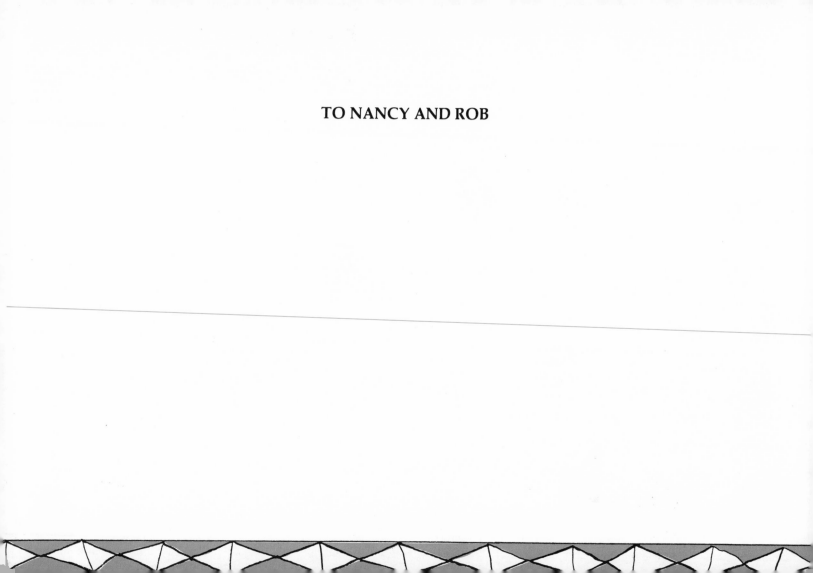

The whites have power given them by Great Spirit to read and write.
He gave us power to talk with our hands and arms,
write with pictures, and send messages with mirror,
blanket, pony far-away, smoke, fire arrows, and flint.

—Sioux Chief Iron Hawk

INDIAN SIGN LANGUAGE

The Plains Indians had no newspaper or even a written language. However, five years after General George A. Custer and all his personal command were killed in the famous battle of the Little Bighorn, on June 25, 1876, the red man's side of the story was told in hand and arm gestures by Sioux Chief Red Horse, who fought in the battle.

Fortunately, Dr. Charles E. McChesney, acting assistant surgeon of the United States Army, wrote down this story-without-words of Red Horse. His diagrams and detailed descriptions of the signs are the basis for *Chief Red Horse Tells About Custer.*

Indian sign language was the first language generally understood in North America. History records that Columbus and other early explorers used signs in communicating with the native American Indians. The Plains Indians made greater use of signs than other tribes because they were not agricultural people with permanent settlements. They came in contact with tribes speaking different languages as they roamed the western plains in search of the buffalo, which provided them with food, shelter, and clothing.

Because Indian sign language is a simple language, words of similar meaning are expressed by the same sign. One difference between the Indian sign language and the gesture language of the deaf-mutes may be illustrated by the word *think.* The deaf-mutes place extended fingers of the right hand against the forehead. The Indians, on the other hand, believed that thinking came from the heart and made a sign pointing to the heart. Perhaps nothing can give so complete an understanding of the feelings and beliefs of these early Americans as a study of their sign language.

Indian sign language is easily learned because the signs are mostly natural ways of expressing ideas. Many people today use some gestures or signs when speaking to make their meanings clear. A person will beckon with his finger to say *come* or wave his hand outward to say *go*. Here are examples of sign language used by the Plains Indians:

Say or *tell*— Pass the palm of the hand slightly outwards from the chin.

Listen or *hear*— Cup hand behind the ear.

See or *look*— With the index and second fingers parted and pointing ahead, hold one hand just below one eye.

Walk or *run*— Move the hands, palms down, alternately one before the other, as feet would move. The same sign made more rapidly means *run*.

Sioux or *Cutthroats*— Draw hand across neck as though cutting the throat.

White man—Draw the index finger across the forehead where the hat brim would be.

Soldier or *warrior*— Bring closed fists in front of breast, thumbs touching, before separating fists to each side.

Many or *plenty*— With fingers curved, raise hands in front of body and swoop them together as though gathering up something.

HISTORICAL BACKGROUND

The settlement of the West was hindered by powerful Sioux and Cheyenne tribes defending their land. Therefore, in the treaty of 1868 between the Indians and the United States government, the Indians were given the huge Dakota Territory as a reservation. Forts were built to confine them from the whites. However, when gold was discovered in the Indians' sacred Black Hills, thousands of white people overran the Siouan hunting grounds.

Between 1875 and 1876, buffalo became so scarce that the government allowed the Indians to leave their Black Hills reservation and hunt in the Bighorn country of northern Wyoming. When ordered to return to the reservation, which was no longer a hunting ground, the Indians refused.

Sitting Bull, the chief medicine man of the Hunkpapa Sioux, wearing his colorful tribal dress, went to President Grant in the White House and begged for "trade, not aid." He asked that the trade terms in their treaty be carried out so that their land would be restored to them. Grant listened, then he presented a beautiful new rifle to the chief, but instead of promising to protect the Indians' land, Grant tried to bargain for more Sioux territory.

Disappointed and angry, Sitting Bull returned home and sent messengers to all the roving camps asking for a council at Tongue River. There he organized an army to protect Indian rights and drive out the white man by force. According to Sitting Bull, the whites clearly wanted war, and they should have it. He urged, "Let us have one big fight with the soldiers."

Anger flamed between the white man and the Sioux. To meet the Indian threat of war, the U.S. Army ordered the 7th Cavalry Regiment to clear out the Sioux. General George A. Custer, a rash and headstrong veteran of the Civil War, commanded an advance guard that was ordered out against the Teton and Dakota Sioux. General Alfred H. Terry was expected to join Custer with the main body of the troops on June 26, 1876.

On June 24, when Custer arrived near an Indian village in the bend of the Little Bighorn River in Montana Territory, he believed he faced a small party of Indians. Custer was overly ambitious and decided to disregard Terry's orders. On June 25, he divided his soldiers into three groups and set forth to surround the Indians. He sent one group, under Colonel Frederick W. Benteen, to explore the territory south of the river bend. Another group, under Major Marcus A. Reno, Custer sent to approach the Indian camp along the west bank of the river. Shortly, however, after the loss of 56 men, Reno was forced to retreat to a high bluff. Benteen, hearing fire, hastened to Reno's assistance, and their combined forces held off the Indians until Terry's forces arrived the next day.

Meanwhile, Custer had sped forward with the third group of soldiers. What happened to him is history. The "small party" Custer had expected turned out to be the full strength of Sitting Bull's warriors. Gall, a powerful chief of the Hunkpapas, attacked him. Within an hour, Custer and his entire division of around 260 men lay dead on the field. Not one white man lived to tell of the battle.

Unknown to the whites, Sitting Bull's forces of 6,000 or so outnumbered the total white soldiers in the area by ten to one. His superior number of warriors, fighting in their hit-and-miss fashion, defeated Custer's forces in the greatest victory of Indian history.

After Custer had been wiped out in the Battle of the Little Bighorn, the Indians refused contact with the remaining white forces and scattered. Sitting Bull himself surrendered to the United States in 1881. Most of the Sioux Indians drifted back to their reservation in Dakota. Many of them settled in the Bighorn Mountains.

GLOSSARY OF INDIAN TERMS USED IN THIS BOOK
(listed in order of occurrence)

Five little grasses ago	Five springs (years) ago
Red Cloud Tepees	Cheyenne Agency
Cutthroats	Sioux
Good River	Cheyenne River
Greasy Grass Creek	Little Bighorn River
Sitting Bull's Warriors	Hunkpapas
Different White Man Soldiers	Custer's troops
White Man Soldiers on Hill	Reno's forces
White Man Soldier Chief	General Custer
Knife Tribe	Santees

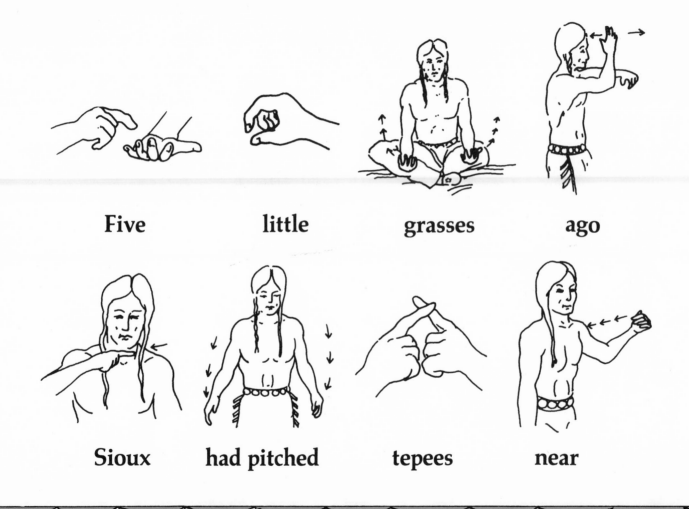

Five   **little**   **grasses**   **ago**

Sioux   **had pitched**   **tepees**   **near**

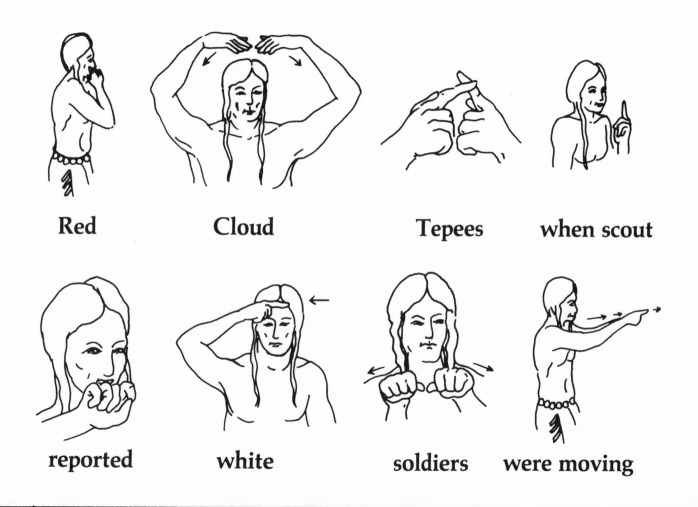

Red   **Cloud**   **Tepees**   **when scout**

reported   **white**   **soldiers**   **were moving**

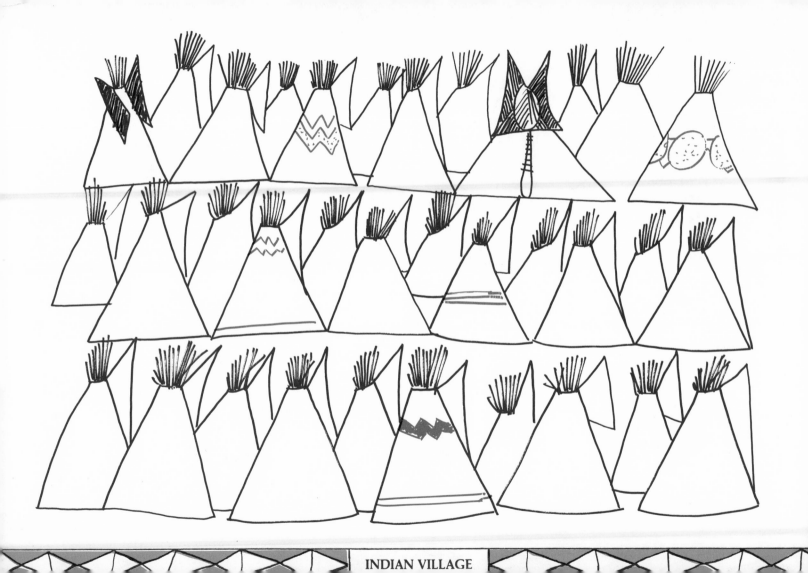

INDIAN VILLAGE

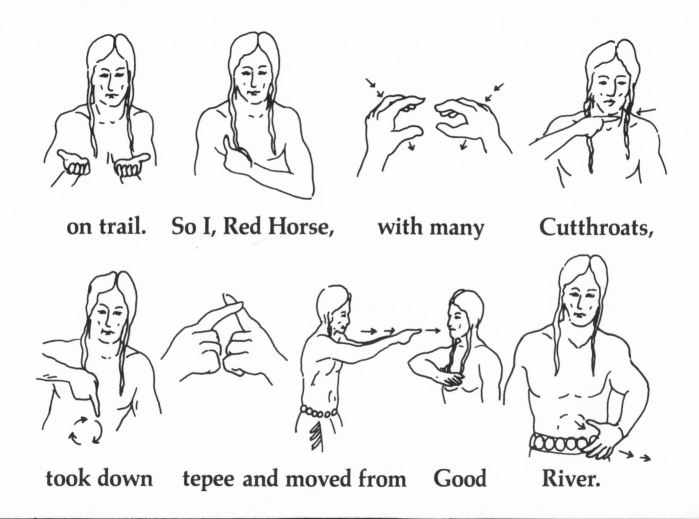

on trail.   So I, Red Horse,   with many   Cutthroats,

took down   tepee and moved from   Good   River.

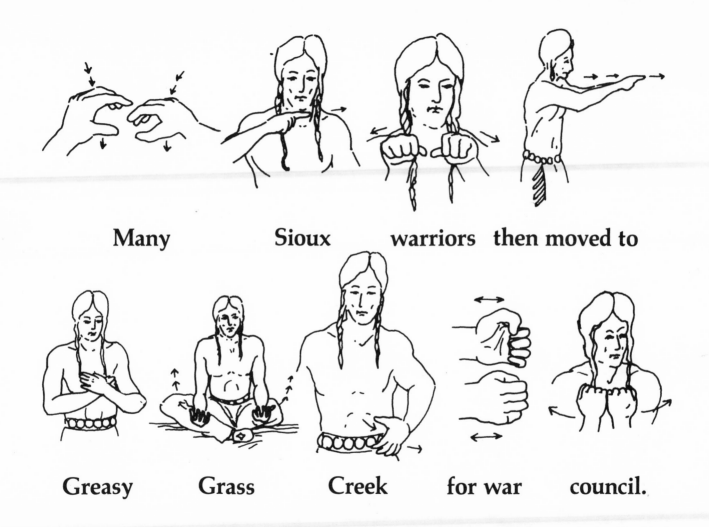

Many   Sioux   warriors then moved to

Greasy   Grass   Creek   for war   council.

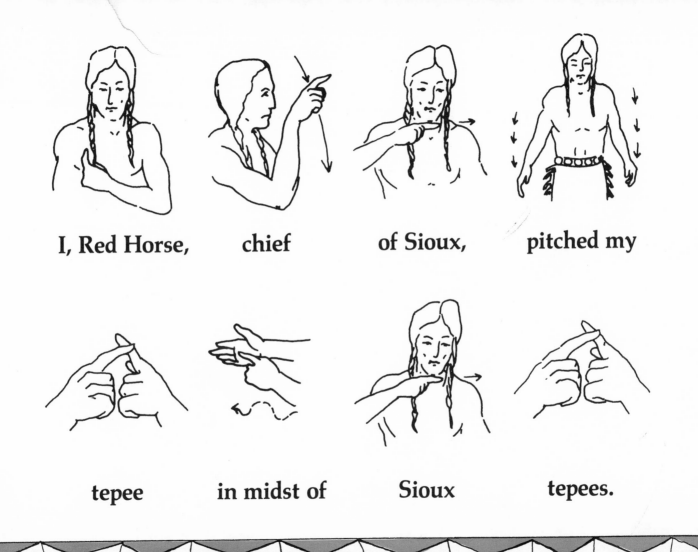

I, Red Horse,   **chief**   **of Sioux,**   **pitched my**

tepee   **in midst of**   **Sioux**   **tepees.**

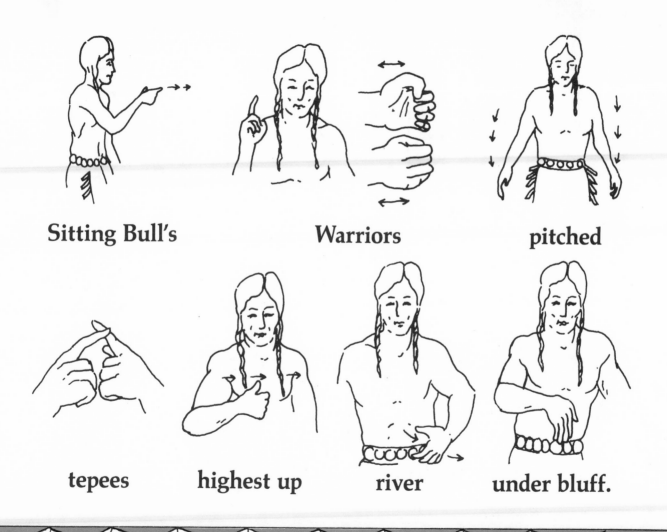

Sitting Bull's   **Warriors**   **pitched**

tepees   **highest up**   **river**   **under bluff.**

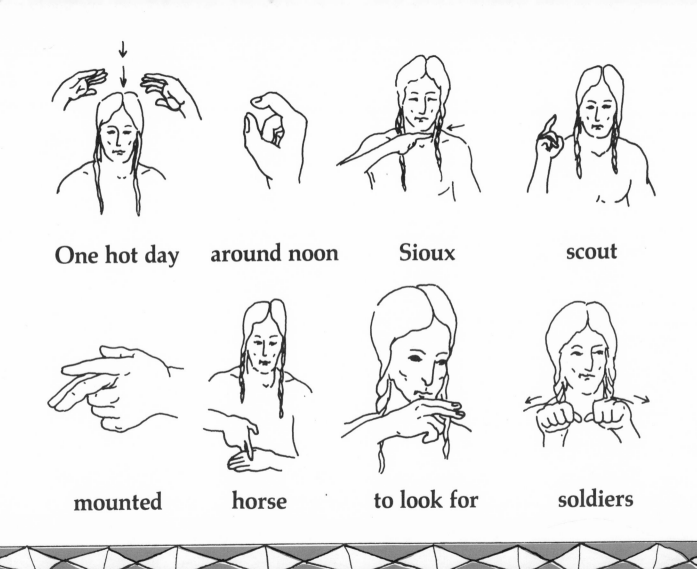

One hot day   **around noon**   **Sioux**   **scout**

mounted   **horse**   **to look for**   **soldiers**

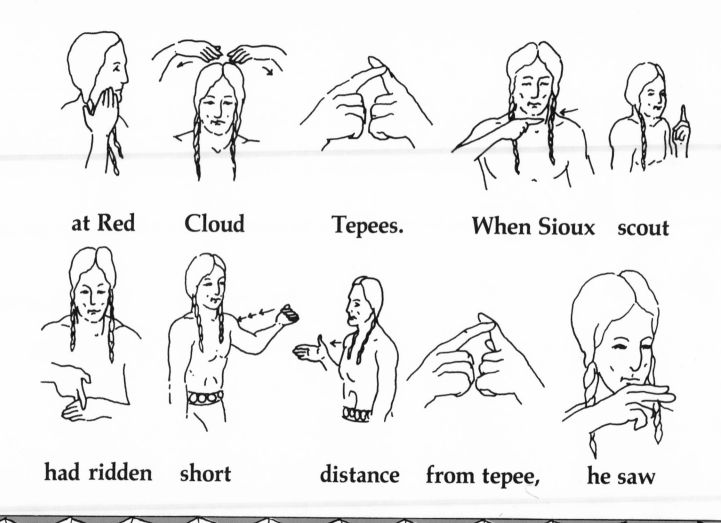

at Red   Cloud   Tepees.   When Sioux   scout

had ridden   short   distance   from tepee,   he saw

cloud of dust rising. He turned back   and said,   "I think

many   buffalo   are moving   near."

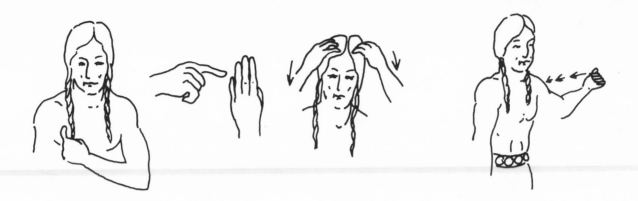

I, Red Horse, and four   women   were short distance away

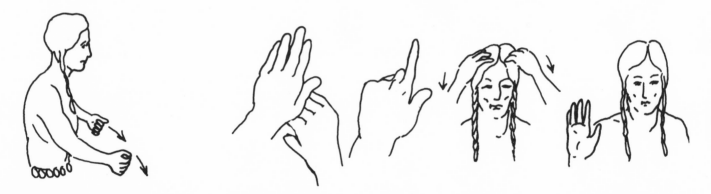

digging wild turnips.   Suddenly,   one   woman   pointed to

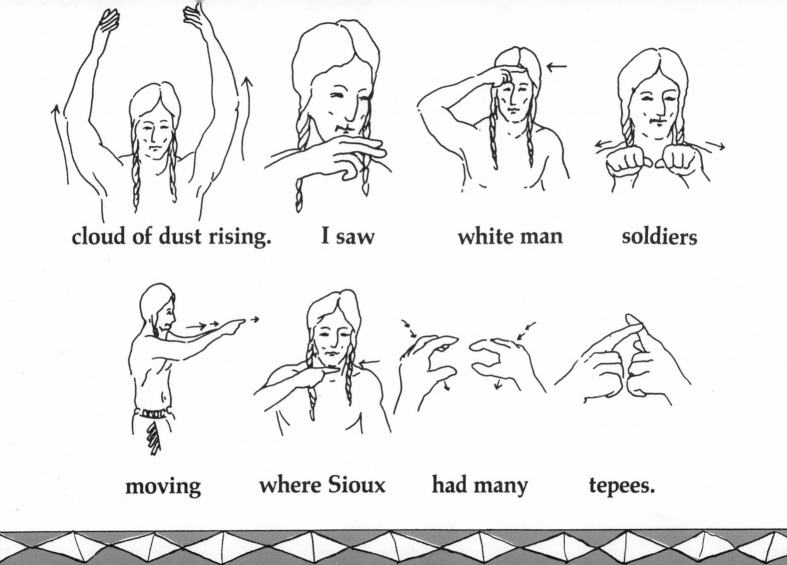

cloud of dust rising.   I saw   white man   soldiers

moving   where Sioux   had many   tepees.

SOLDIERS APPROACHING VILLAGE

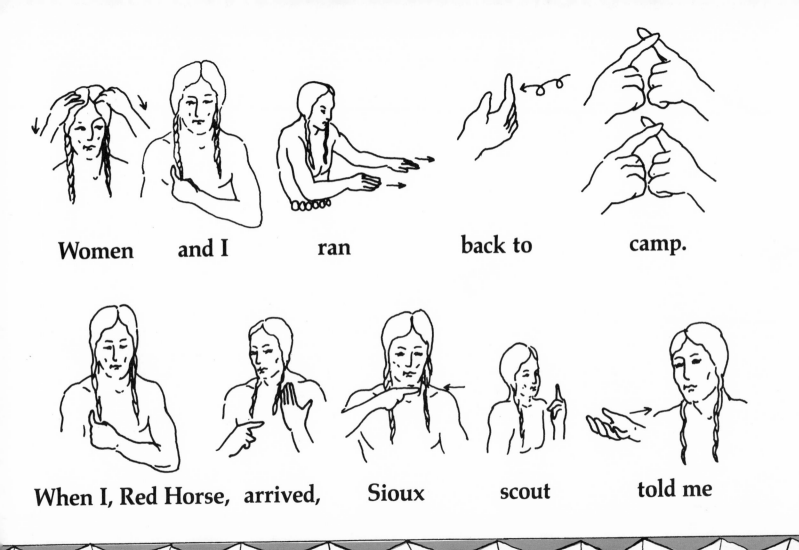

Women   **and I**   **ran**   **back to**   **camp.**

When I, Red Horse,   **arrived,**   **Sioux**   **scout**   **told me**

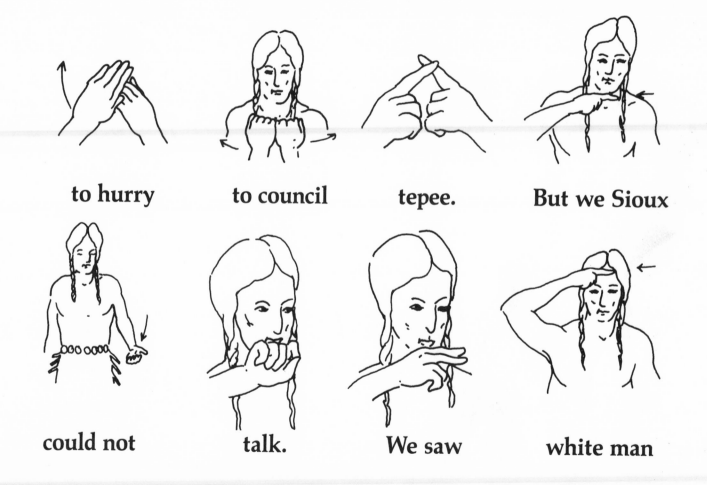

to hurry   to council   tepee.   But we Sioux

could not   talk.   We saw   white man

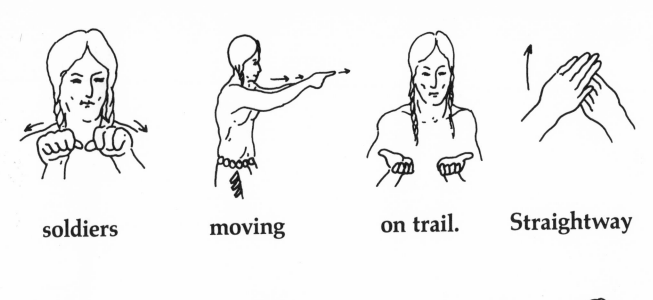

soldiers   moving   on trail.   Straightway

we ran out of   council   tepee   in all directions.

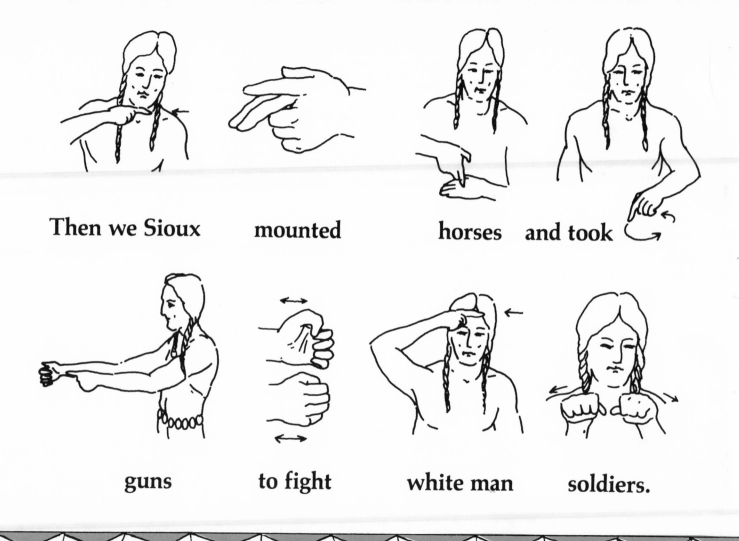

Then we Sioux   **mounted**   **horses**   **and took**

guns   **to fight**   **white man**   **soldiers.**

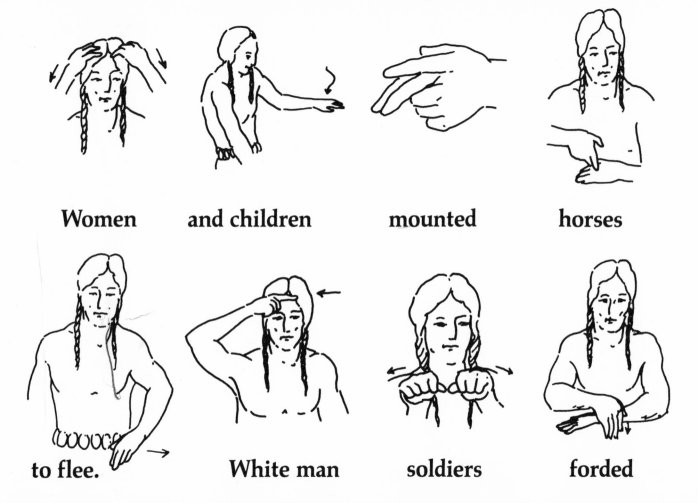

Women   **and children**   **mounted**   **horses**

to flee.   **White man**   **soldiers**   **forded**

Greasy   **Grass**   **Creek**   **farther up than**

Sioux   **had crossed**   **and fought**   **Sitting Bull's**   **Tribe.**

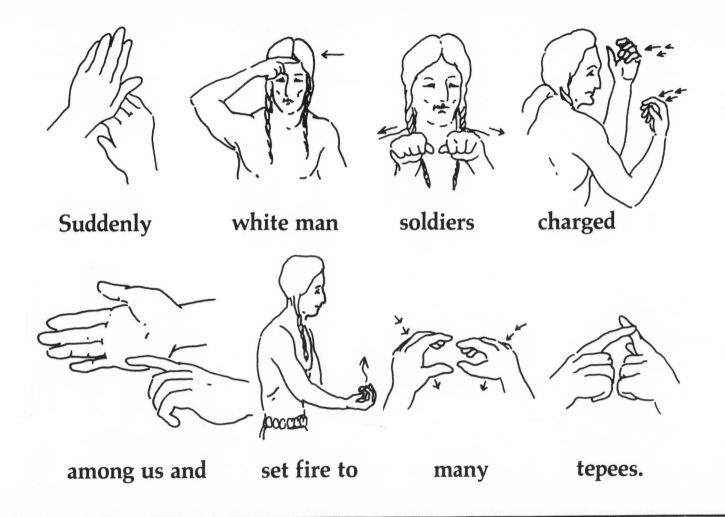

Suddenly   **white man**   **soldiers**   **charged**

among us and   **set fire to**   **many**   **tepees.**

INDIANS CHARGING SOLDIERS

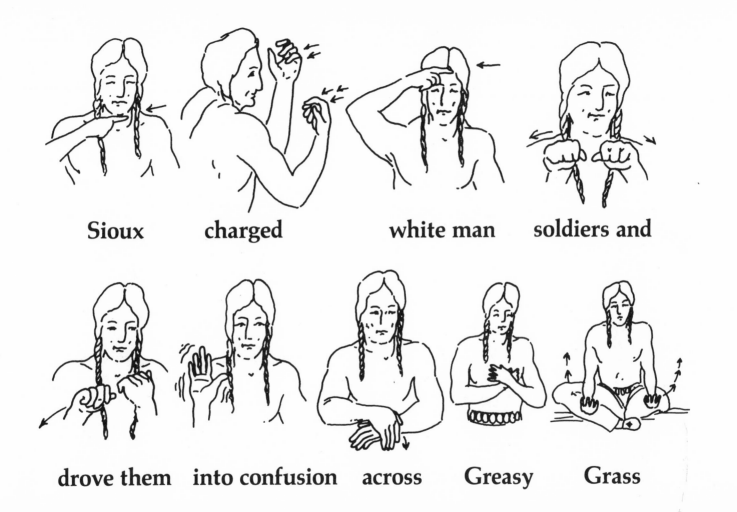

Sioux   **charged**   **white man**   **soldiers and**

drove them   **into confusion**   **across**   **Greasy**   **Grass**

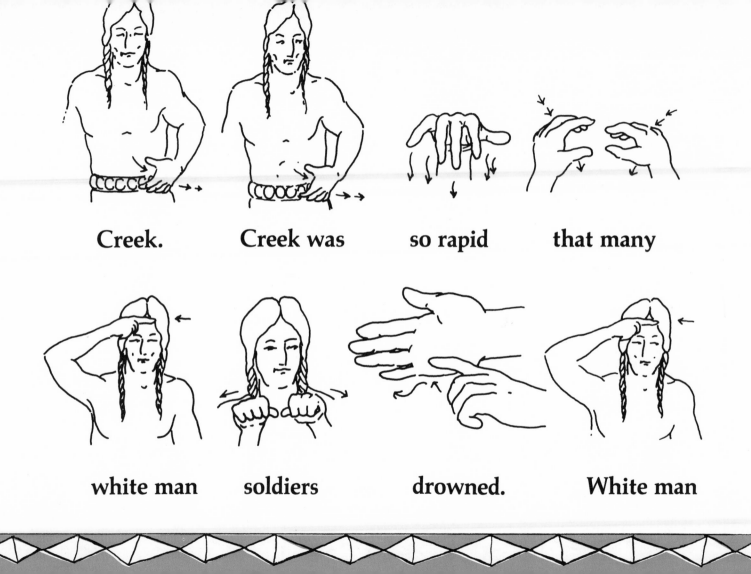

Creek. **Creek was** **so rapid** **that many**

white man **soldiers** **drowned.** **White man**

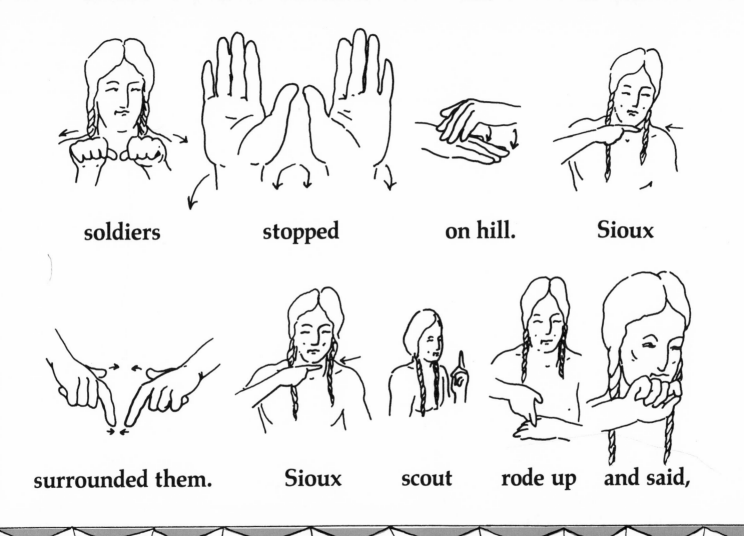

soldiers   **stopped**   **on hill.**   **Sioux**

surrounded them.   **Sioux**   **scout**   **rode up**   **and said,**

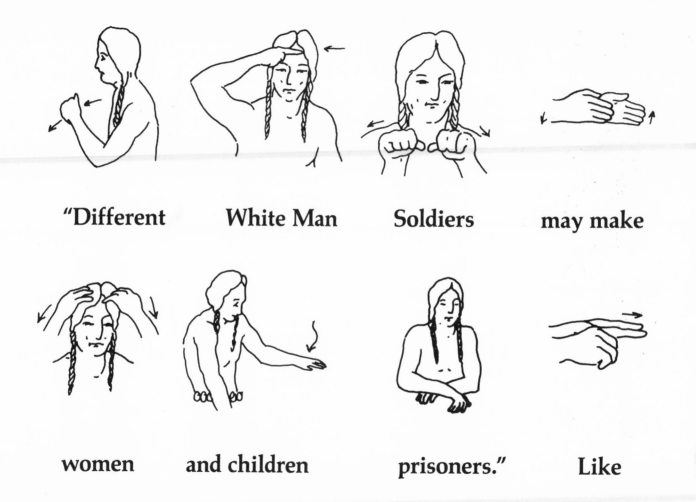

"Different   White Man   Soldiers   may make

women   and children   prisoners."   Like

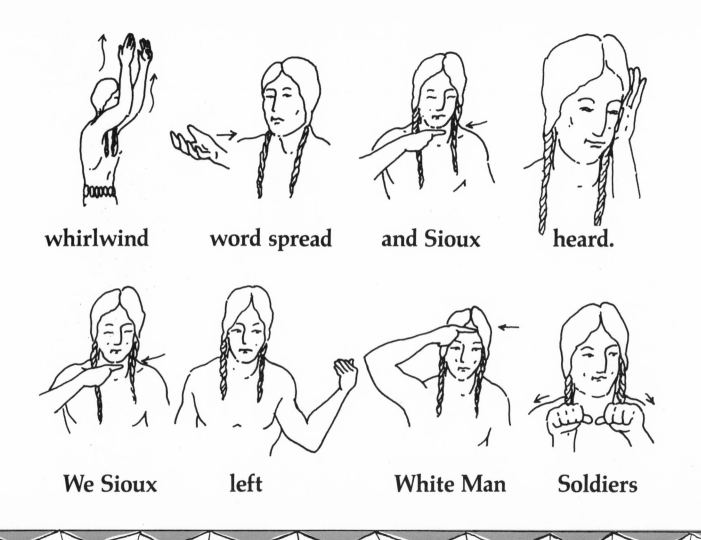

whirlwind   word spread   and Sioux   heard.

We Sioux   left   White Man   Soldiers

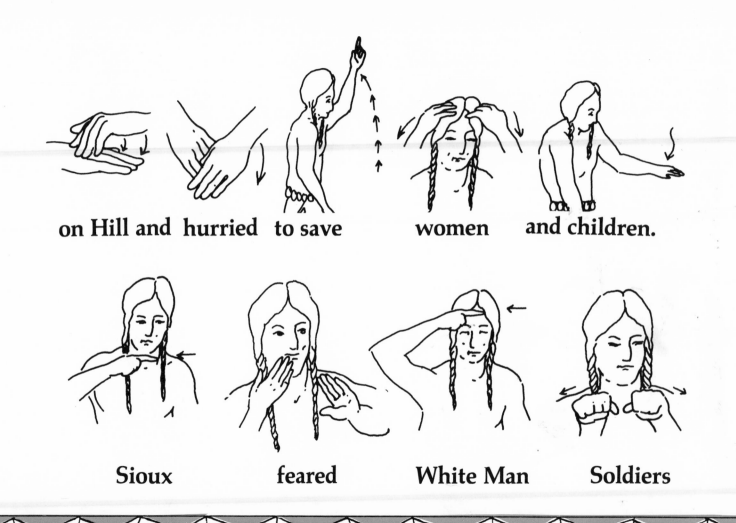

on Hill and hurried to save   women   and children.

Sioux   feared   White Man   Soldiers

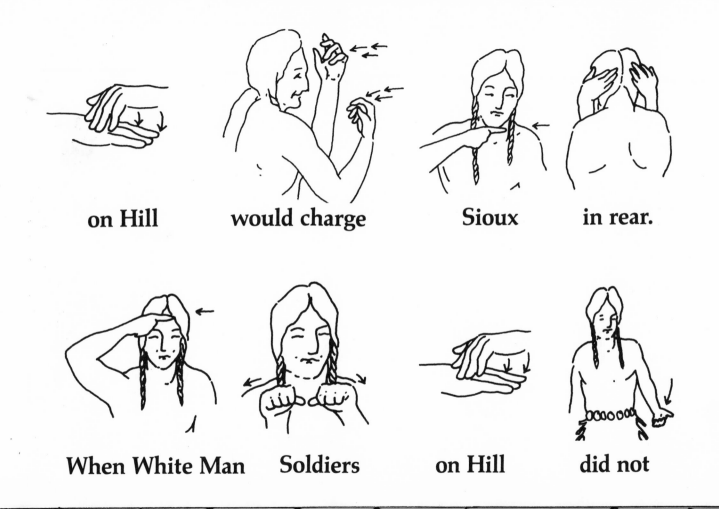

on Hill   would charge   Sioux   in rear.

When White Man   Soldiers   on Hill   did not

charge,   **Sioux**   **thought**   **they had**   **no cartridges.**

On level   **ground**   **by creek**   **I, Red Horse,**   **saw**

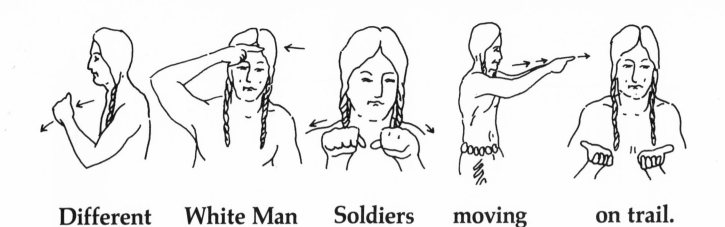

Different   **White Man**   **Soldiers**   **moving**   **on trail.**

In front of   **soldiers,**   **White Man**   **Soldier**   **Chief**

was riding horse with feet like snow.

White Man Soldier Chief had long

hair,   big-brimmed hat, and deerskin clothes.   White Man

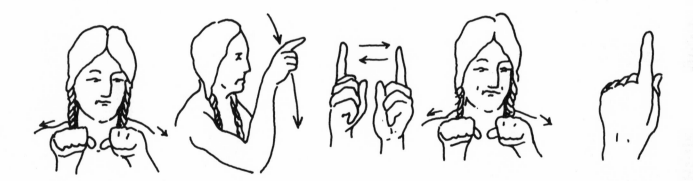

Soldier   Chief   had divided   soldiers.   One

CUSTER'S COLUMN FIGHTING

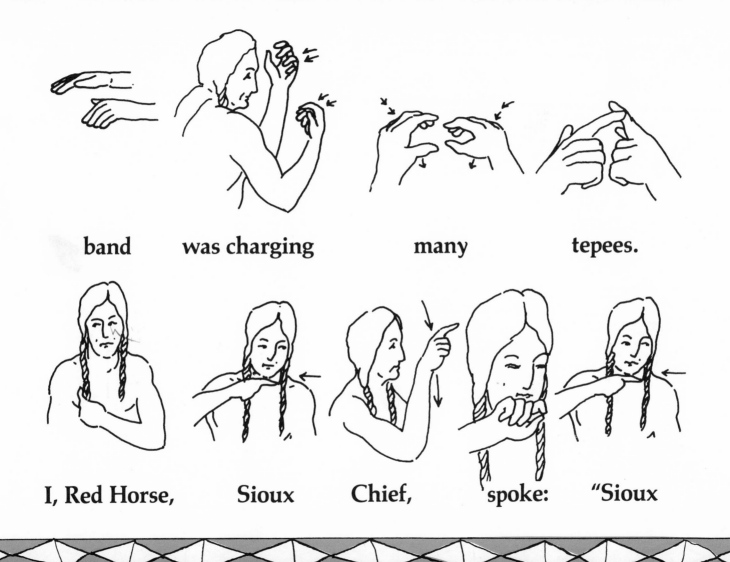

band   was charging   many   tepees.

I, Red Horse,   Sioux   Chief,   spoke: "Sioux

warriors,   watch   White Man   Soldiers   on Hill.

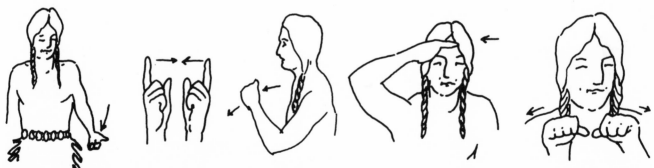

Do not   let them join Different   White Man   Soldiers."

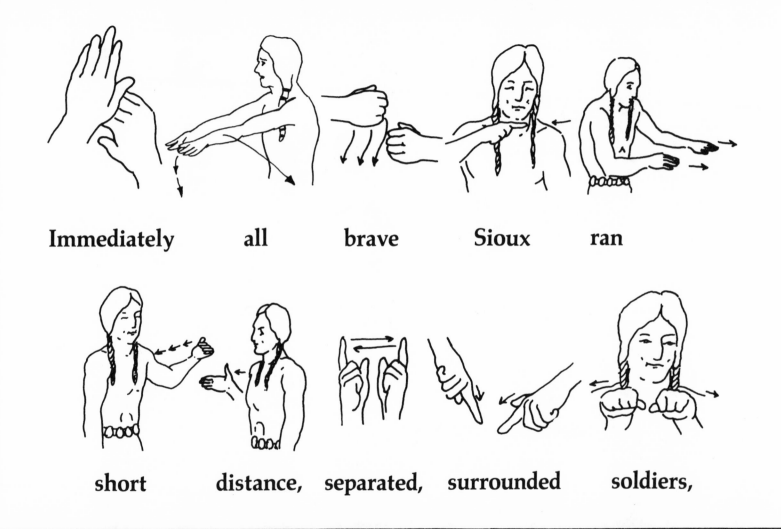

Immediately   **all**   **brave**   **Sioux**   **ran**

short   **distance,**   **separated,**   **surrounded**   **soldiers,**

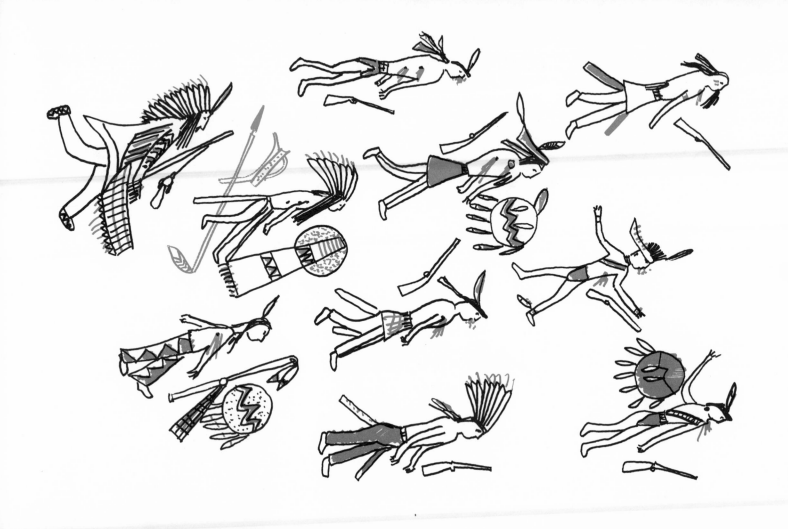

SIOUX KILLED BY CUSTER'S COLUMN

and charged   to save   women   and children.

Brave   **Different**   **White Man**   **Soldiers**   **fought**

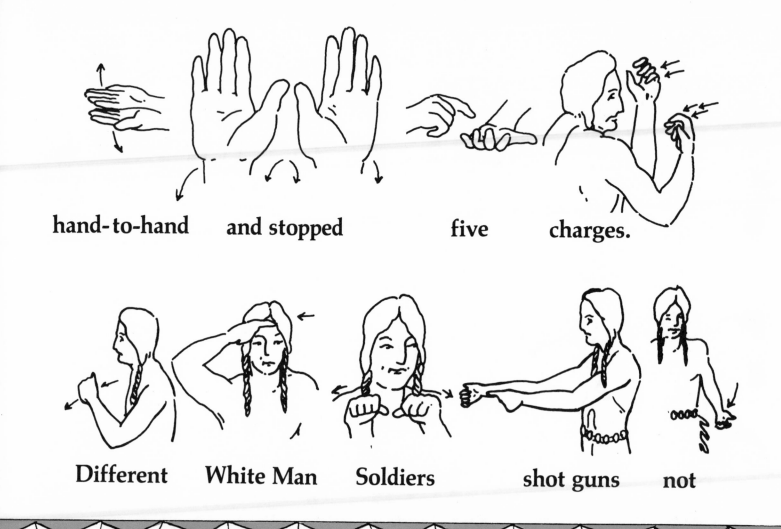

hand-to-hand   **and stopped**   **five**   **charges.**

Different   **White Man**   **Soldiers**   **shot guns**   **not**

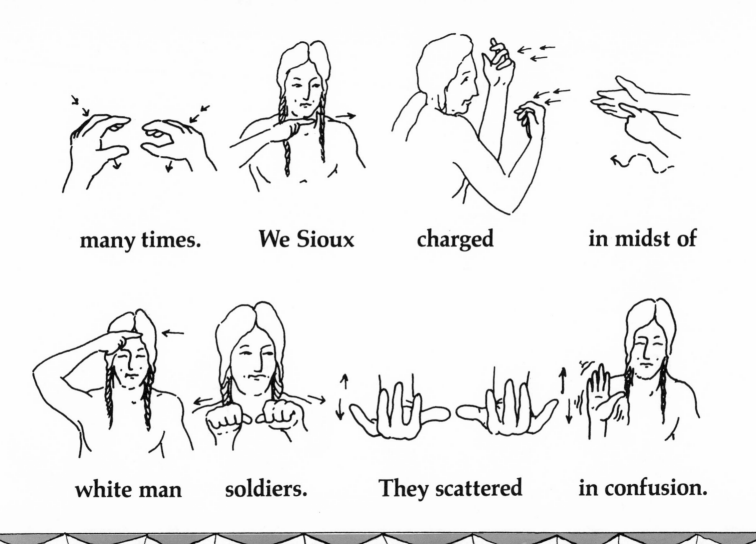

many times.   We Sioux   charged   in midst of

white man   soldiers.   They scattered   in confusion.

CUSTER'S COLUMN RETREATING

Different   **White Man**   **Soldiers**   **became foolish.**

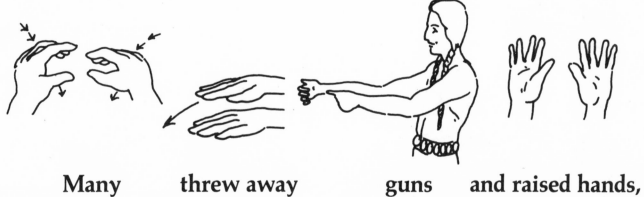

Many   **threw away**   **guns**   **and raised hands,**

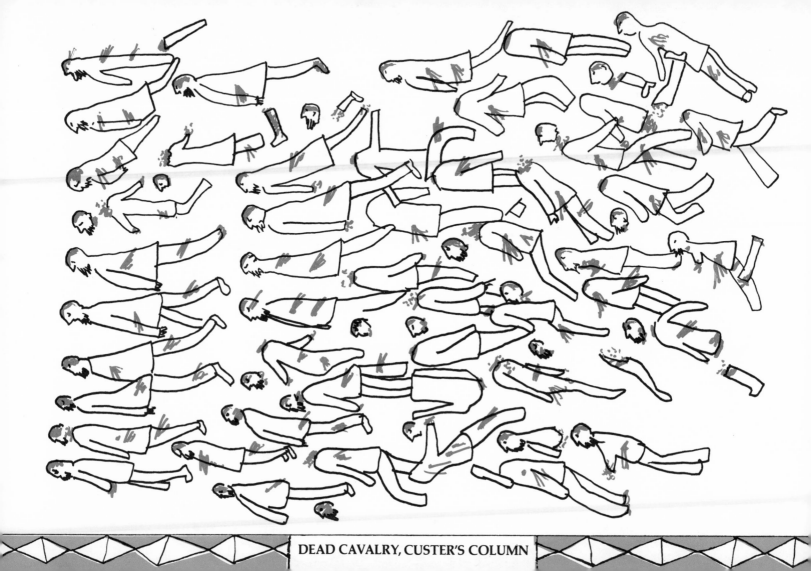

DEAD CAVALRY, CUSTER'S COLUMN

saying, "Sioux, make us prisoners." By custom,

Sioux did not take one prisoner.

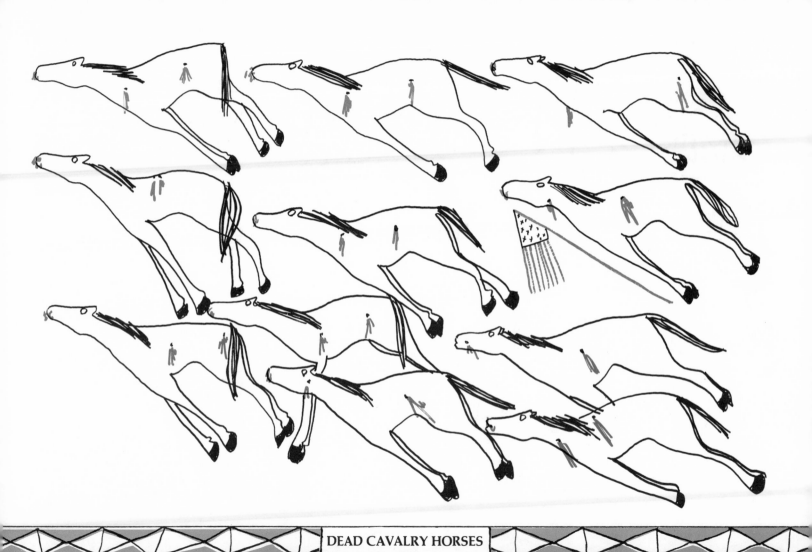

DEAD CAVALRY HORSES

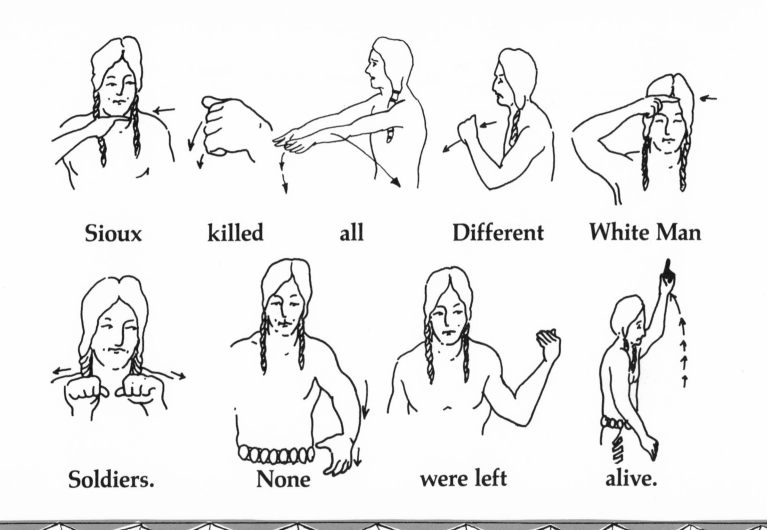

Sioux   **killed**   **all**   **Different**   **White Man**

Soldiers.   **None**   **were left**   **alive.**

I heard   **Sioux**   **say:**   **"White Man**

Soldier   **Chief**   **saved**   **many**

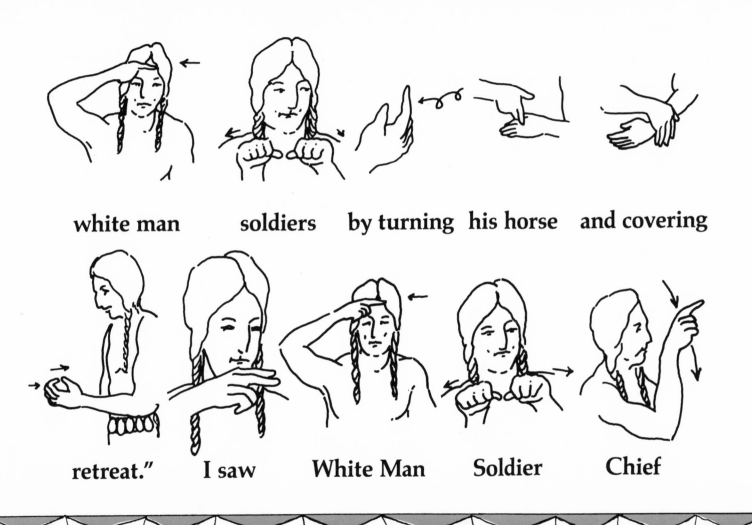

white man   soldiers   by turning   his horse   and covering

retreat."   I saw   White Man   Soldier   Chief

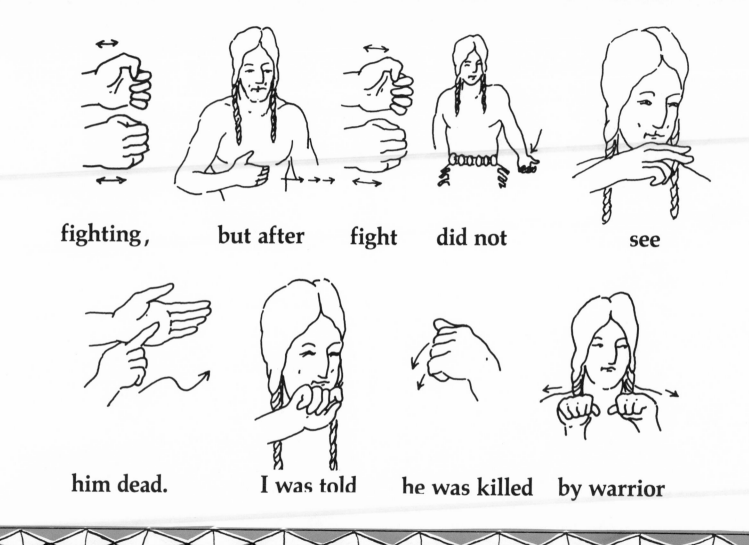

fighting,   **but after**   **fight**   **did not**   **see**

him dead.   **I was told**   **he was killed**   **by warrior**

of Knife Tribe, **who took** **horse.** **Sioux**

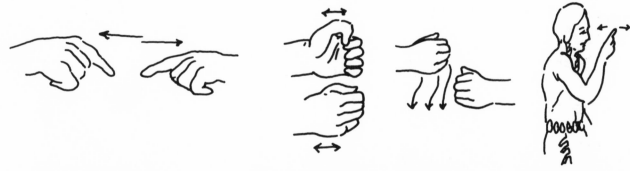

for long time **have fought** **bravest** **of various**

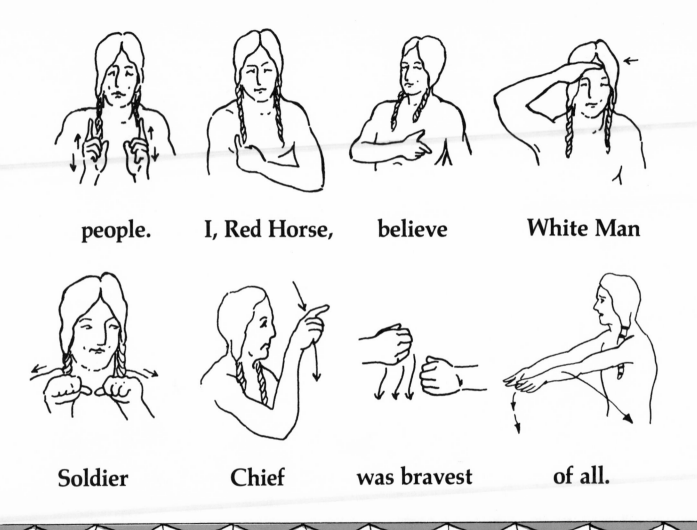

people.   I, Red Horse,   believe   White Man

Soldier   Chief   was bravest   of all.

INDIANS LEAVING THE BATTLEGROUND

ABOUT THE AUTHOR

"Several years ago," says author Jessie Brewer McGaw, "while searching for Indian pictographs at the Smithsonian Institution, I was shown by the curator of the American Ethnology section some material that had lain in the files since 1888. This neglected material has been the basis for this book."

CHIEF RED HORSE is Mrs. McGaw's fourth pictographic book, the results of a lifelong interest in language arts. A teacher of Latin and English in Nashville and Houston for nearly thirty years, she is now retired, but she contributes her time as a volunteer, helping foreign students at the University of Houston. She has one daughter and two grandchildren, and she lives in Houston in a beach house near the Gulf of Mexico.